C

The Lamplighter's Funeral

Garfield's Apprentices

LEON GARFIELD

The Lamplighter's Funeral

illustrated by
ANTONY MAITLAND

HEINEMANN
London

William Heinemann Ltd
15 Queen Street, Mayfair, London W1X 8BE

LONDON   MELBOURNE   TORONTO
JOHANNESBURG   AUCKLAND

First published 1976
© Leon Garfield 1976
Illustrations © Antony Maitland 1976

434 94032 1

Printed and bound in Great Britain by
Morrison & Gibb Ltd., London and Edinburgh

To Jane

At half past after eleven o'clock (by the great bell of Bow),
of a cold, dark October night, a coffin came out of Trump
Alley, with six figures in white to shoulder it and a river of
fire to light it on its way. Smoke pouring upwards heaved
and loitered between the second and first floor windows of
the narrow tenements, so that those looking down saw, as it
were, a thick, fallen sky dimly pierced by a moving crowd
of flames.

"It's heathen," said one soul whose parlour had filled up
with smoke. "Why can't they go by daylight, like decent
Christians?"

Slowly, and with much jolting (the bearers were of
unequal height), the coffin turned right and lumbered
down St Lawrence Lane in the wake of the marching fire.

7

"I wish you long life," said an old Jew to a coffin-bearer he knew by sight; and a little crowd on the corner of Cheapside uncovered as fifty lamplighters, all in white jackets and black cocked hats, filed across the road and turned into Queen Street with torches blazing and stinking the night out with fumes of melting pitch.

In accordance with old custom, they were burying one of their number whose light had been eternally put out two days before, in consequence of an inflammation of the lungs. One Sam Bold, lamplighter of Cripplegate Ward, having providently joined the burial club and paid his dues, was now being conducted with flaming pomp to his last snuffing place in St Martin's Churchyard. Although he had been a solitary man, such was the brotherhood of the lamplighters that any death among them made more than a small hole in the night; their yellowed faces were dull and sad. . . .

One in particular looked sadder than all the rest, not from any extreme of grief, but because, having a chill himself and thinking too much of the fate of Sam Bold, he had taken a good quantity of gin to keep out the murderous cold air. The night had hit him hard, and he felt dizzy. Already the cobbles of Cheapside had almost overturned him; as he got into Queen Street he caught his foot against a rift in the pavement and went down in a shower of sparks and blazing pitch, like a comet of doom.

A crowd of street urchins who had been following Sam Bold's fiery progress to the grave, screamed with unseemly excitement while the lamplighters tramped grimly on. Then one child—more perilous than the rest—darted forward

and picked up the still burning torch. A slender, skinny-
fingered child with eyes as round as hot pennies . . .

The torchlight lit his face so that it seemed transparent
with fire and floating in the smoke. The fallen lamplighter
gazed vacantly at the apparition; then, overcome with
shame at his fall, tried to explain:

9

"Issa f-funeral . . . muss go on. Respect . . . feel awful. . . ."

The child stared down.

"I'll go. . . ."

"No . . . no. 's not proper. Wouldn't be 'spectful. . . . Oh I feel awful. . . ."

"I'll be respectful . . . reely."

"You sure?"

"Cross me heart."

"Take me—me jacket, then. Muss wear the p-proper jacket. It's the rule. And me 'at. Proper f-funeral 'at. Give 'em back later. . . ."

The dazed lamplighter struggled out of his jacket; his hat lay in the street beside him.

" 'ere! P-put 'em on. Muss be 'spectful. Issa f-funeral. . . ."

The white jacket engulfed the child and the hat finished him off so that the lamplighter had the weird feeling he had attired a ghost that had just departed, leaving the empty clothes standing, stiff with terror. A sleeve reached out and took up the torch again.

"I'll be respectful," said the invisible child, and tipped back the hat sufficiently to uncover the seeing portion of his eerily solemn face.

The coffin had already passed on, and the deputy lamplighter had to scamper and run, with flame streaming, till he caught up with the funeral by St Thomas the Apostle and took his place among the marchers.

At last Sam Bold was laid to rest in St Martin's Churchyard and the deputy lamplighter acquitted himself with dignity and respect. He stood stock still amid the great crescent of fire that lit up the open grave and, with due solemnity after the black earth had thumped down, quenched his torch in the bucket provided—as did all the other brethren of the lamp—with the honourable words: "A light has gone out."

In the oppressive darkness that followed this general putting out, the company of mourners fumbled their way down Church Lane to where a funeral feast was awaiting them at the Eagle and Child. This was the custom; each man paid towards the coffin, and what was left over provided for meat, cakes and ale.

The Eagle and Child was an elderly inn that hung over the river like the glimmering poop of a ship that had taken a wrong turn and sailed among houses. . . . One by one the mourners climbed up the wooden steps that led to the overhanging bay where the feast was laid out. Last of all came the deputy, not wanting to disgrace the occasion by hanging back.

The president of the burial club, who collected shillings at the door, held out his hand. For a moment there was a stillness in nature as to him who expected there was nothing given; the deputy did not possess a shilling. The president frowned, then observing the white jacket and cocked hat, took the occupant of them for Sam Bold's son. The dead man having been of Cripplegate ward and he of Bishopsgate, they had not been personally known to one another. For all the president knew, Sam Bold had a dozen sons, and this before him was the representative of them all. He withdrew his expectant hand and gestured the orphan through the door. One didn't demand a shilling off a bereaved child.

Inside the parlour, the talk was generally what it always is after a funeral: quiet, with a discreet cheerfulness breaking in; not everyone can be struck to the heart by one man's death. As the ale went down, spirits went up, and there was singing, of a gentle sort . . . nothing rowdy or quick; such songs as "Sally in our Alley", or "Over the Hills and Far Away".

After a little while the deputy lamplighter joined in, not wanting to be conspicuous by keeping silent; his voice was high and singularly sweet. Several of the older brethren quietly shed tears, thinking, like the president, that here was Sam Bold's orphan, bearing up wonderfully. None liked to ask where his mother was, for fear of opening old wounds if, as was likely, she turned out to be dead.

At half past midnight there was a commotion on the steps outside, as of many feet struggling against incomprehensible odds. The president went to open the door and the lamplighter who'd fallen in Queen Street appeared in a dusty and confused condition. After greeting the company, he searched out his deputy and recovered his jacket and hat.

" ''ad a good feed, lad?" he inquired, gesturing towards the remains of the feast.

The lad, thin and bitterly ragged, looked up and shook his head.

"Not so much as a drop or a crumb," said someone, not understanding the deputizing arrangement and still taking the child to be an orphaned Bold. "It's only to be expected," he went on. "No appetite. Next of kin, you know . . ."

The new arrival—whose name was Pallcat—looked muddled. The child plucked him aside.

"I didn't like to say . . . I didn't have no shilling. . . . And it was only till you came. . . . I'll go now—"

Pallcat, not yet his usual miserly self, felt in his pockets for a coin.

"I don't want nothing," murmured the child awkwardly. "Reely."

Instantly Pallcat took his hands out of his pockets.

"Wodger do it for, then?"

"I was sorry for you. . . ."

Pallcat stared down disbelievingly.

"What's yer name?"

"Possul."

"Possul? That ain't a name," said Pallcat.

" 's after St Thomas the Apostle, where I does odd jobs."

Totally mystified, Pallcat scratched his greasy head, which reeked of the fish oil that supplied the lamps.

" 'ave a cake," he said at length. " 'ave a piece of pie and a thimble of ale. 's all right. I paid me dues . . . and I ain't up to eating meself."

Possul gravely thanked his benefactor and drank and ate. Then there were more songs and Possul obliged the company with "While Shepherds watched", sung solo until he got to "and glory shone around," when the company softly joined in, as became a congregation of lamplighters.

At half past one, the last of the candles supplied by the landlord of the Eagle and Child went out and the funeral party departed into the moonless night, pausing at the foot of the steps to shake each other by the hand and get their hazy bearings from the watermen's lights that still flickered and danced on the black river.

"Where d'you live, Possul?"

"Over Shoreditch way."

"With yer ma and pa?"

Possul shook his head vigorously and Pallcat fancied he'd half smiled. (Queer, that, thought Pallcat for a moment.)

"I got rooms in Three Kings Court," he said, blinking to clear his brain. "Just back of Covent Garden."

Possul gazed at him in admiration.

"Two rooms," went on Pallcat, moved to a foolish boasting. "You can come back with me if you like—"

The invitation just slipped out. Pallcat's heart sank as he heard his own voice oozing hospitality. He could have bitten off his tongue. He hoped Possul hadn't heard him. . . .

"Don't want to be a trouble to you."

"No trouble," snarled Pallcat. "'s a pleasure."

The journey back to Three Kings Court was full of corners and carpings, as Pallcat roundly cursed the lamp-lighters of those wards and parishes who'd been too dis-honest to fill their lamps to last out the night.

"Issa sacred dooty," he kept saying as blackness engulfed them. "Issa Christian office to lighten our darkness. And it's a wicked 'eathen thing to give short measures and sell the oil what's left."

Pallcat's drunkenness kept coming over him in waves; and whenever it went away he felt very cold and couldn't keep his eyes off skinny Possul to whom he'd offered a bed for the night.

Why, in the name of all the saints, had he done such a thing? It wasn't like him. What if Possul *had* helped him out and said nothing to the lamplighters about the shameful circumstance that had made it necessary? He, Pallcat, had fed him for his trouble. Surely that was enough? He glared at Possul whose face was bright with expectation. "You ought to be on your knees and thanking me," thought Pallcat, irritably.

The smell of ancient cabbage and trodden oranges stole upon the air as they neared Covent Garden. Pallcat had always lived alone, and had steadily improved himself by having no other soul to provide for. He worked hard, lighting his lamps at sunset and, thereafter, offering himself out as a link-man to light those who paid him the way home.

Such earning a living by shedding light in darkness gave him notions of great importance about himself; it was hard for him not to think of himself as some kind of judge, dividing light from dark—and choosing where and when to shine.

This, combined with a natural meanness, made men say of him that, when his link went out, he charged for the moonlight—if there happened to be any about.

"Second floor back," said Pallcat, as they came to the lofty tenement in Three Kings Court where he lodged.

His room stank so much of fish oil that the smell seemed to come out and hit the visitor like an invisible fist. Within there was a sense of bulk and confusion that resolved itself, when he turned up a lamp, into all the wild and tattered furnishings he'd bought between the setting and the rising of the sun. Tables, chairs, chests, commodes, pots and jugs, together with a quantity of glass cases containing stuffed birds and cats, were collected in meaningless heaps like the

parts needed for the first five days of creation. There was
also dust in plenty; it was not hard to believe that Pallcat
himself had been formed out of it.

"'ome!" said Pallcat, and, taking a taper from the lamp,
lit another. The oil-stained walls appeared—between
obstructions. Possul gazed at them in wonderment. Framed
texts hung everywhere; some were burned into wooden
panels, some were crudely stitched onto linen, as if by
Pallcat himself.

"I AM THE LIGHT OF THE WORLD," said one; "HE THAT FOLLOWETH ME SHALL NOT WALK IN DARKNESS."

"THE TRUE LIGHT WHICH LIGHTETH EVERY MAN," proclaimed another.

"GOD SAID, LET THERE BE LIGHT," hung over the foot of Pallcat's bed; "AND THERE WAS LIGHT," hung over the head.

"HE WAS A BURNING AND A SHINING LIGHT," was propped above the fireplace; and "LIFT UP THE LIGHT OF THY COUNTENANCE," was nailed over a mirror that was tarnished like a disease.

"There's a couch in t'other room," said Pallcat. "You can sleep there."

They slept away what was left of the night; they slept on through the grey and rowdy morning. Pallcat awoke some time after noon. Confused memories kept coming back to him, and he closed his eyes against the daylight that contrived to be as soiled as the windows. He recollected that he had company. Possul's weirdly transparent face, floating in smoke as when he'd first seen it, appeared before his inner eye. Then he remembered that Possul had carried the funeral light when he'd fallen by the wayside; that made some sort of bond between them.

He opened his eyes and gazed at his stuffed beasts which had been arranged so they might look back at him and reflect himself in their glass eyes. " 'All is vanity and vexation of the spirit,' " he mumbled; and pricked his ears.

The rooms were still. The thought struck him that Possul had already gone and, possibly, robbed him into the bargain. He crawled from the chaos of his bed and poked his head into the next room. Possul lay on the couch, breathing regularly. Being a child, he took sleep in greater quantities than a grown man.

Pallcat felt vaguely displeased; then he felt vaguely disappointed. He'd caught himself hoping that Possul, moved by the kindness and hospitality shown him, would have cleaned the room and prepared a meal while he, Pallcat, slept. But no such thing. The boy was ungrateful, like all boys. His angelic countenance and soft manners were things he'd picked up in the church where he'd worked; they were no more part of his deep nature than would have been a wig or a new hat.

He went out to get some food, determined to make the boy ashamed of himself for allowing a grown man to wait on him. When he came back, the boy was still asleep. Pallcat stared long and hard at his small, pale face, and had thoughts about shaking him till his teeth flew out; instead, however, he went into the next room and made a great deal of noise preparing to go out on his duties. He kicked against his oil can, dropped his wick trimmers and flung the lock and chain that secured his ladder to a banister rail with a heavy crash onto the floor. In spite of

D74165

this, Possul did not wake up. Pallcat wondered if he was ill? He went back and laid an oily hand on the boy's forehead, and then touched his own; there was no great difference in heat. He bent down and blew gently on the child's face.

Possul frowned, stirred and turned over with a sigh. Pallcat snarled and departed on his sunset task.

His lamps were in the Strand, stretching on either side from Charing Cross to St Mary's; also there were three each in Bedford and Southampton Streets, making four and twenty in all. High on his ladder, Pallcat tended them, filling the tins with oil, trimming the wicks, kindling them

and giving the thick glass panes a dirty wipe before descending and passing on to the next. From each lamp he took the greasy, burnt remainder and afterwards sold it to the boot-boys for blacking hats, boots and iron stoves. In this way he extended his dominion; he gave light by night and black by day.

In itself his task was humble, but when Pallcat was mounted up some twenty feet above the homeward hastening throng, and saw that the daylight was going, he felt as remote and indifferent as the kindler of the stars.

When he returned to Three Kings Court it was already dark; the kindler of the stars couldn't help feeling warmed by the thought of company. Possul was awake and sitting on the end of his bed; he hadn't so much as lifted a finger to clean or tidy anything. Pallcat put down his empty oil can.

"I'd ha' thought," he grunted, "you'd ha' done *something* —'stead of just sitting and waiting."

"Didn't like to," said Possul, widening his peculiarly bright eyes. "Might have done something wrong."

"I left food out," said Pallcat, baffled.

"Saw it," said Possul. "Didn't like to eat any, though. Just had some water."

"Too idle to eat, even," muttered Pallcat. "You'll 'ave to mend your ways if you stay 'ere."

Possul nodded and mended his ways to the extent of eating what had been provided. The lamplighter watched him half indulgently, half irritably; the boy ate everything, without asking if he, Pallcat, wanted any. He wondered how much nourishment it was expected of him to provide.

"If you are going to stay," he said harshly, "you'll 'ave to *do* something for it."

Possul, his mouth so full that a piece of jellied veal was hanging out of it, looked up with bright, earnest eyes.

"I'll learn you," said the lamplighter grandly, "to be me apprentice. Now a lamplighter's apprentice is, very properly, a link-boy; that is, a nipper what lights the night folk their way 'ome. I done it meself—and I still do it; it's a 'oly thing to do. 'And the Lord went before them . . . by night, in a pillar of fire, to give them light.' "

" 'The true light, which lighteth every man,' " read Possul, off the wall.

" 'Arise, shine; for thy light is come,' " said Pallcat,

handing the boy a length of tow that had been dipped in pitch.

" 'I was eyes to the blind, and feet was I to the lame,' " said Possul, reading from a text that was still in the stitching stage.

"But not," said the lamplighter, making for the door, "without proper payment. Pitch costs money and tow don't last for ever."

They went downstairs into the dark, cold court and walked to the Strand and along to the corner of Dirty Lane where there was a coffee-house with gambling rooms above. Here Pallcat kindled the torch.

"I'll show you," he said, holding up the burning article so that his reddened eyes streamed from the sudden clouds of smoke.

Possul gazed at the lamplighter whose flame-lit countenance resembled an angry planet in the gloom; then his eyes strayed to Pallcat's lamps that winked in the obscure air down either side of the Strand. It took sharp eyes to make them out, they glimmered so feebly within the accumulated filth of the glass that enclosed them. Although they complied with the letter of the law and burned from sunset to sunrise, they mocked the spirit of that law and provided not the smallest scrap of illumination. If ever a world walked in need of light, it was the world under Pallcat's lamps.

"Light you 'ome," shouted Pallcat, brandishing the torch before a gentleman who came stumbling by.

"No—no. I can see, thank you."

"Fall in the river and drown, then," said Pallcat to the gentleman's departing back.

He accosted several other passers-by, but none wanted light, so Pallcat damned them all; at the same time he shielded his torch lest a stray beam might have given an advantage not contracted for.

"D'you see? Like this! 'Stretch out thine hand . . . that there may be darkness over the land, even a darkness which may be felt.'"

At length, three gentlemen came out of the coffee-house. Their aspect was mellow, their gait airy.

"Light you 'ome?" offered Pallcat.

"And why not?" said one of the gentlemen, affably.

"A link-man with his spark!" said another, observing the boy beside the lamplighter. They all laughed and gave Pallcat lengthy directions to their homes.

Pallcat walked on ahead, holding the torch high; Possul took it all in, walking beside the lamplighter and occasionally raising his own arm in what he regarded as a professional way.

Presently Pallcat became aware that they'd attracted a non-paying customer, a wretched, gin-sodden devil who was lurching along, taking advantage of the free light to avoid the posts and projecting steps with which the streets were endlessly obstructed.

"Watch this," muttered the lamplighter to his earnest spark. "This is the way we does it."

Pallcat took off his hat and, waiting for a sharp corner, whipped it before the torch, thus neatly plunging the stinking drunkard into an eclipse. There was a thump and a staggering crash as the wretch collided with a post and fell with a howl of pain.

" 'Cast out into the outer darkness,' " said Pallcat powerfully; " 'there shall be weeping and gnashing of teeth.' "

After that they were troubled no more and the three gentlemen, deposited in their homes, each gave Pallcat a sixpence for the guidance. Pallcat bit the coins and stowed them in a bag hung round his neck; then he and his apprentice went back to the Strand to see out the rest of the night.

Shortly before dawn, when Pallcat's torch was becoming superfluous, he and Possul returned to Three Kings Court. On the way the lamplighter pointed out those corners and alleys where pitch might be had, for a farthing a dip when a man's torch had burned through.

Before going to bed, Pallcat made Possul a bowl of soup, feeling, at the same time, that the boy ought to be waiting on him. But no doubt that would come in time. Possul was simple-minded; he needed careful training—like a dog. And when all was said and done, he *was* company. . . .

For an hour or so after Possul was asleep, Pallcat stitched away at his unfinished text, which was always his bedtime pleasure and task, and somehow made his world seem larger; then he too went down as the blaring sun came up and rendered his room a mad and dirty horror of too-visible confusion.

They slept the day through; Pallcat woke first and went out for food and more oil. When he returned he found Possul sitting peaceably on his bed, having done nothing but wake up.

"Tonight," said the lamplighter peevishly, "you'll work, my lad."

Possul smiled contentedly and Pallcat could have clouted him with the length of tow that was to be his torch. The boy should have *offered*, instead of just waiting to be told, with his bright eyes going right through Pallcat like a pair of pokers.

"You go where we was last night. I'll go more towards Charing Cross. 'ere's a penny, 'case you run out of pitch before you gets paid. Remember what I showed you; remember about keeping your light for the lawful customers. Best take me cocked 'at; only don't scorch it."

Possul, feeling immensely important—as became his occupation of link-boy—flamed outside the coffee-house on the corner of Dirty Lane. The warmth of his torch kept out the bitterness of the night, and his transparent seeming face made a hopeful island in the black pool of Pallcat's hat.

"Light you home, ma'am?" he called out to a flower-cheeked woman who hobbled the street with eyes like cups of ashes.

"Shove off!" she said, and shrank from the damaging light.

Next, a pair of basket-women approached.

"Light you home, ladies?"

They drew near, smilingly shaking their heads.

"Just come for a warm, love."

They held up their hands and drenched them in the heat
of Possul's fire. The boy was nonplussed. Light he must not
give without payment; but Pallcat had said nothing about
warmth. On account of the basket-women and several
other freezing souls, Possul lost several likely customers.

All in all, he earned but a single sixpence that night—
and then spent nearly half of it on fresh pitch for his waning
torch. Pallcat was indignant when he'd got over his pleasure
and relief at seeing Possul come back. Though he'd never
have admitted it, he'd been haunted by the dread of Possul

abandoning him as lightly as he'd joined him. He couldn't quite believe that Possul was real; that is, when the boy was out of his sight. . . .

He rated Possul soundly for his extravagance in pitch, and warned him to mend his ways. He sent him off to bed with—as the saying goes—a flea in his ear, which doubtless found company in Possul's horrible bed. Then he set about finishing his text and beginning a new one, especially for Possul: "He that toucheth pitch shall be defiled therewith."

Next night, with many warnings, Possul went out again to set himself up in business on the corner of Dirty Lane. The lamplighter, who accompanied him as far as the Strand, watched him flame his way towards the coffee-house with mingled feelings of suspicion and pride. The boy stalked along with such an air of self-importance that one might have supposed he was holding up the sun and moon and all the fledgling stars.

In truth, Possul had a soul no less than Pallcat; the sense of consequence given by being a minister of light had its effect on the boy no less than the man.

"Light you home, sir?"

"Take me to Clifford's Inn, child. D'you know it?"

" 's off Chancery Lane."

The gentleman nodded and Possul set off. Presently a low noise in a cleft between two houses distracted him. He held out his torch. A woman and nearly naked child were huddled together in an attempt to get warmth from each other. The woman, half blinded by the sudden light, looked savage at the intrusion on her misery. Possul paused, as if to give his gentleman full benefit of the sight.

"Get a move on, boy," he said. "It's no business of ours in there."

Possul withdrew the torch and left the cleft in decent darkness. A little while after, he stopped again. A legless beggar who squatted on a porridge pot and got about by dragging himself by fist and fingernail over the cobbles, squinted up from the entrance to an alley. Every detail of his misfortune was pitiless in Possul's leaping fire.

"Get along with you," said the gentleman. "Find something better worth looking at."

So Possul looked and found a pair of lovers sitting on a doorstep. Furiously they bade him take his light away—which he did to his gentleman's protesting disappointment.

Just outside the gate to Clifford's Inn a youngish woman was humped against a wall and crying. Possul lingered and his torchlight shone on her tear-stained face, revealing harsh bruises and dried blood.

"That's enough," said the gentleman. "When I want to be shown the miseries of the night I'll employ you again. Till then, my lad, keep out of my way."

He gave Possul only threepence and dismissed him. The link-boy had two further customers that night, and, as if by design (though it was not so at all), he led them likewise on pilgrimages through the horror and despair hidden in the dark.

Even as moths are drawn to a candle flame, so was every cruelty and misfortune drawn into the circle of Possul's torch. Or so it seemed. Consequently he got a bad name and each of his customers swore they'd never seek his light again. They'd sooner go home in the dark, relying on the lamplighter's feeble glimmers rather than the link-boy's bitter fire.

When he returned to Three Kings Court at dawn, he looked weary, but nothing to worry about. A night's work naturally wore a soul out. Pallcat took his apprentice's earnings, made him soup and packed him off to bed.

Next night, encouraged by his beginnings, Possul found other customers—and uncannily led them through similar ways, loitering his torch over all manner of luckless sights. Men crying in corners, dead children, thieves lit up in sudden, horrible terror. . . . Human beings everywhere abandoning themselves to a despair that the darkness should have hid, abruptly seen in their crude nakedness.

33

Thus Possul's torch shed its light. . . .

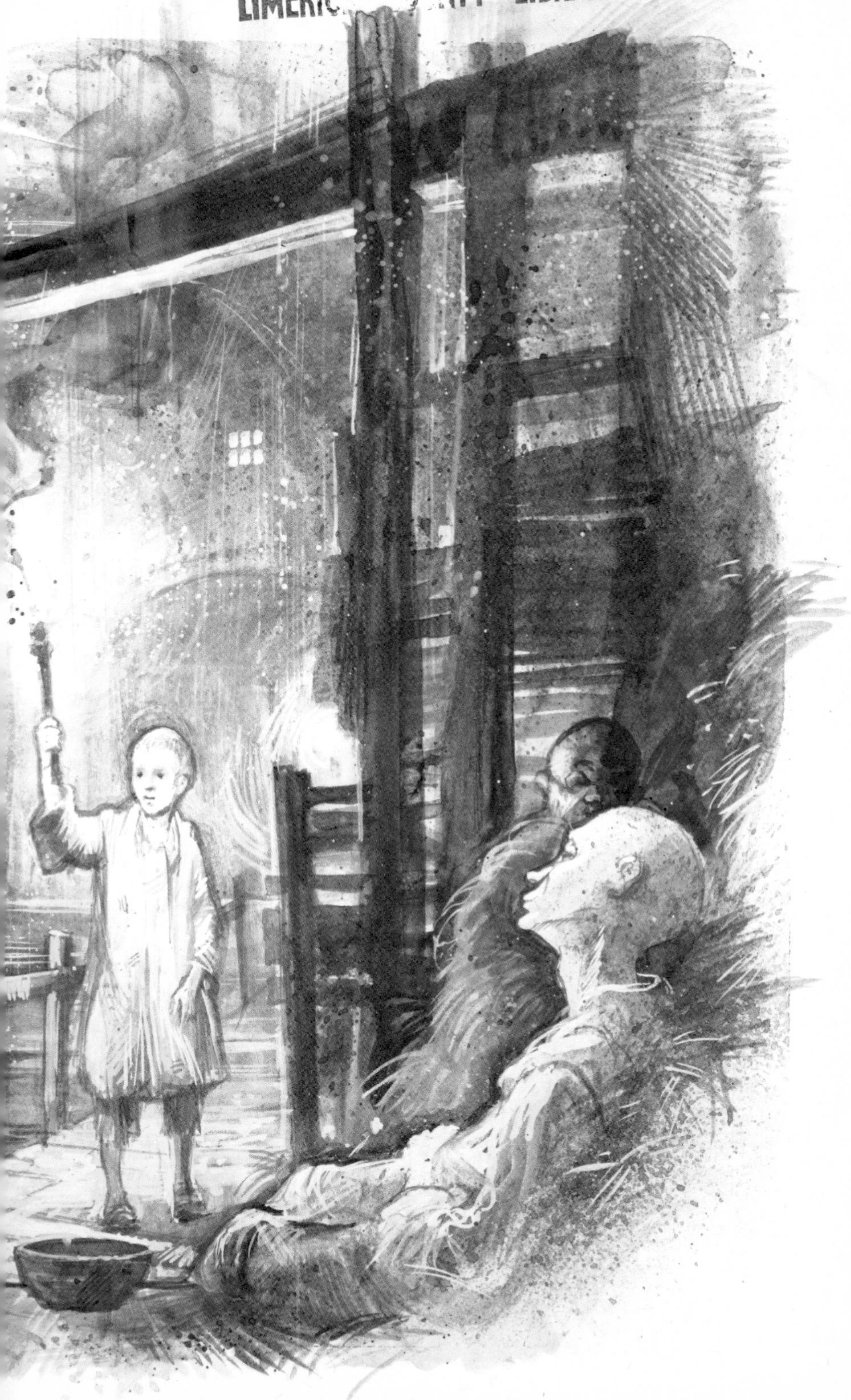

Sometimes it seemed that he took pleasure in what he saw; his face was always so earnest and bright. But no one giving him a second glance and catching his eerily solemn eyes could really credit him with so unnatural a pastime.

Although many of the sights he lit up would have been unremarkable enough by day, by night—picked out of the blackness like little worlds of total hell—they were vile and disgusting. The only explanation was that Possul lacked sensitivity and taste.

Pallcat of course knew nothing of this; Possul never talked much—and then only when spoken to. It never seemed to occur to him that he, Pallcat, had ears that liked exercise. Still, the boy breathed and ate so that one could hear him, and he was a living soul in the lamplighter's dingy lodgings. Pallcat even got a contrary pleasure out of feeding him for no thanks and being taken for granted as an ever-present father. If only, the lamplighter thought, he'd flesh out a bit and not look so shamefully skinny and pale. There was no doubt that, each dawn when the boy returned, he looked whiter and more transparent so that Pallcat had the feeling that sooner or later he'd come back as plain bones.

The lamplighter kept his apprentice on the go for a week; then, on the seventh day, it rained so Pallcat told Possul not to stay out beyond midnight as no one would be about after that.

The rain was not heavy; it was more of a fine drizzle, a weeping of the night air that made the torch hiss and spit and give off smoke in thick bundles. Several gentlemen emerged from the coffee-house, but, having had their bellyful of the loitersome link-boy, waved his offers aside. In accordance with Pallcat's example, Possul wished them in the river. The curse, coming from his soft lips and attended by his bright, earnest gaze, seemed curiously terrible. Yet he uttered it more as if it were a charm to bring him the customers he lacked.

As if in response to this charm, a man came out of the coffee-house on his own. He'd had no experience of Possul so he was not driven to choose darkness instead of light. He was a huge elephant of a fellow, untidily dressed and wearing a frown as if he'd bought it as suiting his particular cast of features. He squinted balefully at Possul's fire.

"Light you home, sir?"

The man grunted ill-temperedly, searching his capacious mind and came out with: " 'Take heed therefore that the light which is in thee be not darkness.' "

He sniffed and wiped his nose against the back of his hand.

"Well?"

"Yes sir. I'll take heed. Where to, sir?"

"Red Lion Square. D'you know it?"

"Off High Holborn, ain't it?"

"Thereabouts. Lead on."

Possul lifted up his torch and went; the large man lumbered after. The rain, although not increasing, had soaked the streets so that the torch, reflecting upon the streaming cobbles, ran along like a river of broken fire. Bearing in mind his customer's strict injunction, Possul kept to the middle of the road and watched where his light fell. He could hear the irritable fellow quite distinctly, muttering and rumbling to himself like distant thunder over the trials of a bad night. The link-boy would be lucky to get a penny from such a man. At last they turned into Grays Inn Passage; the torch flickered across a bundle of rags heaped against a doorstep. As if unable to help himself, the link-boy paused. The huge fellow lurched and swayed to a halt.

"What d'you think you're doing, boy?"

"Nothing—nothing, sir. It's just me torch . . . shining, shin'ng on—" He jerked the light apologetically towards the doorstep. The bundle of rags leaped out of the night; it contained a twig of a woman with arms and cheeks as thin as leaves. She was either dead or so close to it that it would have taken a watchmaker to tell the difference.

Possul remained perfectly still while his torch flames plaited themselves ceaselessly round the melting pitch and fried the soft rain. The huge man's complaints had died away into a heavy sighing; he swayed from side to side as if he found difficulty in managing his bulk.

He carried a stick—a heavy cudgel such as might have been used to beat off a footpad. He poked at the rags with it. There was no response. Possul brought his torch closer to the woman's face. Her skin was blotched and covered with open sores that the rain had made to shine. Her eyelids stirred as Possul brought the fire closer still.

Suddenly a twist of blue flame—no bigger than a finger—danced up above her mouth; then it vanished with extra-

38

ordinary rapidity. It was as if the spark of life had been made visible, departing.

"Get back," grunted the man, pushing Possul away with his cudgel. "She's full of gin. You saw it? That gasp of fire above her lips. The torch set it off. Get away. It's not for you and me to burn her before her time."

He gave Possul another shove, swore malevolently at the night—and bent down, so that every stitch of his clothing protested at the effort. He picked up the gin-sodden, diseased creature as easily as if she'd been a frayed old coat; then he heaved her on his back.

"Move on," he said to Possul.

"Where to, sir?"

"My house. Would you have me carry this unwholesome burden further?"

"What will you do with her, sir?"

"Eat her. Plenty of pepper and salt. Then I'll give her bones to my cat."

The creature that was flopped across his back emitted a raucous moan.

"Peace, ma'am, peace. Presently you'll have comfort and warmth. Hurry, boy, hurry, before we're all poisoned by the stink of her gin."

In a moment, Possul's fire broke out into Red Lion
Square and cast the large man's shadow with its misshapen
double back against the fronts of the stately houses; it
seemed impossible for those within not to feel the dark
passing. Possul himself, holding the torch, cast no such
mark; the intensity of the light seemed to have eaten him
up altogether; to shadow-fanciers, the lurching monster
with the grotesque hump upon its back was quite alone,
save for a steadily marching fire.

Presently the fire and the shadow halted. Then the shadow grew enormous and engulfed one particular house. . . . Cautiously, and with solemn gentleness, the shadow's owner took off his hump and laid the tattered woman against his front door while he fumbled for a coin to pay the link-boy.

Why was the night suddenly so dark? He stood up and turned. The boy with the torch had vanished. The square was empty and without light. He fancied he glimpsed a flickering coming from the direction of Fisher Street, which was some way off. It might have been the light of a link-boy; then again, it might not. The woman at his feet moaned again; he banged ferociously and urgently on his front door. He looked again towards Fisher Street, but the light had gone. He shook his head as if to rid it of a memory that was already faltering into disbelief. His front door opened, but before he went inside, he stared upwards as if for the sight of a new star. Nothing . . . nothing but blackness and rain.

Nor was it only from Red Lion Square that Possul had vanished; he disappeared from Three Kings Court, also.

The night wore out, and Pallcat waited. Time and again he stirred himself and went down into the rain to search the maze of streets about Covent Garden. It was possible that Possul had got lost. Folk often did, round Covent Garden. He went along the Strand and wasted a whole torch in searching. Possul was nowhere to be found. He went back to his rooms. As he mounted the stairs his heart beat in expectation; he crept into Possul's room on tiptoe, almost as if he was frightened that, by making a noise, he'd scare off the fragile dream. He needn't have bothered. He might as well have tramped in with iron boots; the room was empty.

Next morning he went outside again, squinting painfully against the cheap, all-pervasive light. He searched, he inquired, he scavenged in lanes and alleys; he went to the church where Possul had worked. The verger remembered the boy, but had not seen him for many days. Most likely he was dead; it happened sometimes, and mostly to the gentle ones. . . .

Night came on, and, after tending his lamps, Pallcat renewed his search. He carried his torch through street after street, calling now softly, now loudly, for his apprentice. Every darkened alley might have concealed him; but the numerous stirrings and breathings in the night that Pallcat's sharp ears picked up, turned out to be such visions as Possul had lit up, visions of savagery and despair. These hateful and tragic images steadily burned their way into Pallcat's soul, as if the light he served had entered his breast and blistered his heart.

For two nights and days the lamplighter scoured the

town; he scarcely dared return to Three Kings Court on account of the sharp pain of expecting, expecting . . . and then finding only filth, confusion and the emptiness of glass eyes. Possul had vanished, as if off the face of the earth.

At length he went down to the river, which he hated on account of its impenetrable blackness and sense of death. He asked of the waterman if they had seen, had *found* a boy? A thin boy with bright eyes and a transparent seeming face? They had not. But not to give up hope. Often corpses took days to come up and be caught under the bridge. . . .

" 'e weren't real," said Pallcat mournfully. He was in the parlour of the Eagle and Child, in company with two lamp-lighters from Cripplegate Ward. He had given up the river for the night.

On being prompted, Pallcat's companions recollected the boy at Sam Bold's funeral feast, but they did not recall Pallcat going off with him; one thought that the boy had gone off on his own, the other had no clear memories of the latter part of the night.

" 'e never talked much," said Pallcat softly. " 'e were just a—a *presence*. I *felt* 'im when 'e were there; and then when 'e went out I couldn't believe in 'im. 'e 'ad a sort of shining in 'is face. I do believe 'e were a spirit . . . I think."

"What sort of a spirit?" asked one of the lamplighters, with interest. "A angel, p'raps? Some'at of that kind?"

"No . . . no!" said Pallcat, with a flurry of indignation. "A dream in meself. Something made up out of me mind. A spirit like—like—"

"Like gin?" offered the other lamplighter humorously.

Pallcat glanced at him, and the man saw with surprise that Pallcat's old eyes were bright with tears.

"It were a grand dream," said Pallcat, half to himself. "I wish I'd not waked from it, that's all."

He stood up and walked to the window that hung over the river. He brooded on the blackness below, seeing his own face, irregular in the rippled glass, like something floating and drowned.

"I wish," he whispered, "I wish—" when Possul came in.

"*Where you bin?*" screeched Pallcat.

"Found this one with me torch," said Possul, his bright eyes gazing at Pallcat hopefully.

Hanging onto Possul's back, much in the way the wreckage of a woman had hung over the large man's back in Red Lion Square, was an indescribably filthy and gruesome tot—a midget of an infant with a smear of a face and a crust of lousy hair.

"Got him out of the river by Salisbury Stairs. Been looking for his home. Ain't got one—like me. So I thought —I s'posed he'd make another spark?"

Pallcat did not speak, so Possul went on: "I call him 'Stairs', after what he fell in off. Can he come home with us?"

45

Still Pallcat did not speak. The thought of providing for yet another was looming large in his mind; nor could he rule out the possibility of others yet to come. He had seen a light in Possul's eyes such as no lamp had ever given. He could not put a name to it; all he knew was that without it the darkness would be frightful. He gave a little moan. He would have to clean up his rooms; no one else would. He would have to create order out of chaos; no one else would. . . .

"I gave you a fine light, Possul," said Pallcat hopelessly. "And look what you done with it. You must have come out of a winder, Possul; and that's where you'll end up. In a church winder, shot full of arrers. That's what 'appens to saints, Possul; and, all things considered, I ain't surprised. Come on 'ome—the pair of you."

Possul smiled; and Pallcat wondered, not for the first time, which of them was being created in the image of the other?